KU-300-817

Growing Fear

Barbara Mitchelhill

Published in association with
The Basic Skills Agency

Hodder & Stoughton
A MEMBER OF THE HODDER H

Newcastle Under Lyme College

DC028345

Acknowledgements
Cover: Dave Smith
Illustrations: Jim Eldridge

Orders; please contact Bookpoint Ltd, 39 Milton Park, Abingdon, Oxon OX14
4TD. Telephone: (44) 01235 400414, Fax: (44) 01235 400454. Lines are open
from 9.00–6.00, Monday to Saturday, with a 24 hour message answering service.
Email address: orders@bookpoint.co.uk

British Library Cataloguing in Publication Data
A catalogue record for this title is available from the British Library

ISBN 0 340 77599 8

First published 2000
Impression number 10 9 8 7 6 5 4 3 2 1
Year   2005 2004 2003 2002 2001 2000

Copyright © 2000 Barbara Mitchelhill

All rights reserved. No part of this publication may be reproduced or transmitted
in any form or by any means, electronic or mechanical, including photocopying,
recording or any information storage and retrieval system, without permission in
writing from the publisher or under licence from the Copyright Licensing Agency
Limited. Further details of such licences (for reprographic reproduction) may be
obtained from the Copyright Licensing Agency Limited, of 90 Tottenham Court
Road, London W1P 9HE.

Typeset by GreenGate Publishing Services, Tonbridge, Kent.
Printed in Great Britain for Hodder and Stoughton Educational, a division of
Hodder Headline Plc, 338 Euston Road, London NW1 3BH, by Atheneum
Press, Gateshead, Tyne & Wear

Growing Fear

Contents

Fic. Green. MIT.

NEWCASTLE-UNDER-LYME
COLLEGE LEARNING
RESOURCES
DC028345.

1

Hatley Grange

I first saw Hatley Grange last winter.
It was a gloomy house hemmed in by tall trees.
I had read an advert in the paper.
WANTED – Someone to do jobs
around the house and garden.
Six-month contract.
It was just what I was looking for.

I rang the owner – Professor Riffard.
He didn't sound very friendly and snapped,
'Come tomorrow at eleven – and don't be late.'

The house was three storeys high
and built of grey stone.
The gardens were overgrown
with dark leathery shrubs and huge trees.
As I walked up the gravel path
the next morning, I must admit I was nervous.
I reached for the brass knocker
on the oak door and rapped three times.

When the door opened,
I knew it was the professor.
He was tall and skinny and wore a white coat
– just like a doctor.
'Hello,' I said. 'I'm Tom Bradford.'
And I held out my hand.
Instead of shaking it, he said,
'You'd better come in,'
and turned away to walk down the hall.
'I'll show you around,'
he called over his shoulder.
I followed behind him trying to take
everything in. The house was massive.

'This place is in need of a lick of paint,'
he said. 'It's filthy.'
'Right,' I said.
'And the garden needs tidying.'
'I like gardening,' I said.
As he pushed open a green door at the end of
a corridor, a large hairy dog came bounding out.
'Back Franco!' the professor bawled.
'He lives in the kitchen,' he said.
'I keep him as a guard dog.'
Franco didn't look much like a guard dog
to me. He couldn't wait to lick my hand.

'I could take him for walks if you want,'
I said, bending down to stroke him.
'Lisa, the live-in help, does that,' he said.
'You'll meet her later.'

We talked about money.
The wages were brilliant and I could live
there – so no lodging to pay for. Fantastic!
'I want you to start right away,'
said the professor. 'Is that possible?'
No problem. I could hardly wait to move in.

As we walked back down the hall,
we passed a door I hadn't noticed before.
'What's in here?' I asked.
'That's where I work,' he said.
He hadn't told me about his work.
So I asked him.
'I'm a scientist,' he said.
'My work is secret, so no questions –
and stay clear of my lab. That's all I ask.'
I should have done as he said – but I didn't.
That was the trouble.

2

The Laboratory

I started work for the professor the next day.
That was when I met Lisa. She was small
and blonde with a fantastic smile.
'The professor's a bit odd,' she said.
'Brilliant people sometimes are.
I think his work is really important.'
I asked her what it was but she didn't know.
'Don't ask,' she said.

That day, I planned to clear away some of the
dead wood in the garden.
There was a lot of tidying up to be done.

The professor had gone to pick someone up
from the station in the next town.
He'd be away for most of the morning.
'I might as well take Franco out with me,' I said.
'He'll enjoy running about the grounds.'

I had a great time, cutting down old trees
and piling the wood ready to burn.
Franco enjoyed himself too until I saw him
sniffing around the back of the house.
Then he suddenly disappeared
down a cellar grating.
I ran across and saw that one of the bars
in the grate had snapped.
He must have fallen through the gap.
'Franco!' I called. 'Franco, come here boy!'
I stared into the darkness off the cellar.
The dog stood looking up at me,
barking and wagging his tail.

I had to get him out. The professor wouldn't
like me losing the dog on the first day.

I got a metal bar and started
prising open the cast iron grid.
It took me some time but at last I got it out.
I jumped into the cellar to get the dog but
Franco raced away. It was just a game to him.

'Franco, come here,' I called.
I groped along the stone wall for
a light switch. I found it and flicked it on.
As the light flooded the cellar,
my mouth fell open. It was a laboratory.
There were glass cases along one wall,
each containing plants. All carefully labelled.
They were plants like I'd never seen before.
Some were weird.
Each had a chart plotting its growth.

I found Franco behind a bench.
'Good boy,' I said and bent down to grab him.
That was when I noticed the label
on the nearest case. WHEAT.
I looked at the plant inside and stared.
This wasn't ordinary wheat.

This was twice as big as any wheat
I had seen before – maybe more!
Wheat like this could solve the world's
food shortage. Fantastic!

I then remembered the professor's
stern warning.
He wouldn't want me to see his laboratory.
I had to get out.
Any minute now, he'd back from the station.

3

Bad Business

I told Lisa all about it.
'He must be brilliant,' I said.
'Soon there'll be no more starvation
in the world.'
Lisa didn't agree.
'There must be a reason why the wheat's so big.
You must have heard about GM foods, Tom.
They could be dangerous.'
'What's GM?'
'It means *genetically modified*. Changed.
Made to grow bigger or stronger or ...'

'What?'
'Or he could be using chemicals,' she said.
'They could cause diseases.'
I thought she was making a fuss over nothing.
I might have gone on thinking so
if the weather hadn't changed that afternoon.

When it started to rain, I decided to work
indoors. The hall needed painting, so I
started sanding down the skirting boards.
I was crawling along, rubbing away,
when I came to the professor's study door.
I knew he was in there with the businessman
he'd collected from the station.
They were talking. Quite excited they were.
I couldn't help overhearing.

'Take it or leave it!' said the professor.
'Twenty million pounds?' said the businessman.
'I'll have to discuss it
with the members of my board.'
'Just think of the enormous profits
you'll get from the sales.

You'll be producing twice as much as before.
Year after year.'
'It's not perfect yet.'
'It's pretty near perfect.'
'It's risky. If you get caught,
we'll lose everything.'

So the professor was just in it for the money.
Loads of it from the sound of things.
I moved from the door.
I didn't want them to guess
I'd overheard anything.

Lisa was in the kitchen
cooking the evening meal.
I needed to talk.
I went in and I told her everything.

She was stunned.
'You mean the professor's selling GM wheat
for someone to grow in large quantities?'
'Yeah,' I said. 'I'm pretty sure
that's what they were talking about.'

'That's illegal,' she said.
'Perhaps he's just working on developing
some new strains of plants.'
'No,' I said. 'Some of the plants
looked like something from another planet.
Come with me and see for yourself.'
She didn't believe me
but in the end she agreed to go and look.
All we had to do was to wait
until the professor went out.

4

The Rats

NEWCASTLE-UNDER-LYME
COLLEGE LEARNING
RESOURCES

We didn't have long to wait.
The professor soon left
to take the businessman to the station.
We had at least an hour before he returned.
'Right!' I said, as the car disappeared
down the drive. 'Let's go, Lisa.'
We struggled with the grating from the cellar.
Then I jumped down first.
'Come on,' I called to Lisa. 'I'll catch you.'
Once she had landed safely,
I felt for the light switch.

13

'Wow!' she said as the cellar lit up.

'I've got to get a look at these.'

I walked around the cases looking
more closely this time.

Some of the plants I knew.

Oats. Barley. Corn on the cob. Beans.

What was amazing about them was their size.

They were huge!

'Look at those peas,' said Lisa.

'The pods are twice as long as usual.'

'Yeah,' I said. 'So they have twice
as many peas.'

'But they've got thorns!' said Lisa.

'Peas don't have thorns!'

The more we looked,
the more horrified we became.

These plants were not natural.

What would happen if people ate them?

I didn't dare to think about it.

Suddenly Lisa turned her head.

'What's that?' she said.

'What's what?'

'That noise. Over there.'
I stopped and listened. A shuffling noise
was coming from the far side of the cellar.
'Franco's got in,' I said. 'He must be
sniffing around. I'll go and look.'
That part of the cellar was in darkness
until I found another switch.
'Franco!' I yelled as the lights came on.
But it wasn't Franco making the noise.

I stood frozen to the spot when I saw
what was in front of me.
Three large metal cages …
Inside each one was a black rat –
twice … three times as big as usual.
One had three ears. Another had no fur.
The third had eyes caked with yellow pus.
Huge teeth jutted from their mouths
and spittle dripped from the corners.
These rats looked vicious.
I shivered at the sight of them.
'Don't panic, Tom,' Lisa said, calmly.
'You're safe. They're in cages remember.'

Lisa went over and read the labels.
'They're on a special diet,' she said.
'Some kind of new growth hormone.
Just think what a cow would look like
if it had this stuff for dinner!'
Lisa shook her head in disgust.
'He's been working on ways of increasing
growth – no matter what happens.
This is a disaster waiting to happen.'
'We've got to do something, Lisa,' I said.
'Before he sells this stuff.'

5

No Evidence

We decided we'd better talk to the police.
I told the officer everything.
The plants, the rats …
even about the conversation I'd heard.
But I don't think he believed me.
'I'll pop by later,' he said.
'I'll have a word with the professor.
I'm sure there's a simple explanation.'
'No!' I said. 'You don't understand.
He's dangerous.
He'd kill you rather than lose ten million
pounds.'

That did it!

'Ah well, sir,' he said. 'Just let us know
when you've got some evidence to show us.
I'm sure we'll be very interested.'
And he put the phone down.
So much for the police!

'But he was right,' said Lisa.
'You could be playing a joke.
We haven't got any evidence to show them.
Why should they believe us?'
'Then we'll have to get some,' I said.
'How?'
'We could take photographs,' I said.
'Have you got a camera?'
As it happened, Lisa had a Polaroid.
The sort where the photos
are developed right away. Perfect.

'We'll go into the cellar
as soon as we can,' I said.
'We might be in luck tomorrow,' Lisa said.
'Riffard said he was going to the bank.'

We had just decided that this was a good plan
when we heard the professor's car pull up.
We heard the front door open.
'I'm back' he said.
'And I've got some news for you.'

He looked cheerful.
His meeting with the businessman
must have gone well, after all.
He walked towards us, smiling.
'Things have changed,' he said.
'I'd planned to stay here for six months –
but I've decided to move abroad.
I'll give you both two months' salary
but I want you to leave tomorrow morning.'
'Can't we help you pack up?' Lisa said.
'What's the hurry?' I added.
The professor didn't like that.
'I said I want you out!' he barked
and his face flushed with crimson.
'Is that clear?'
I looked at Lisa and she stared back at me.
Now how could we get the evidence?

6

Night Visit

'We've got to stop him,' I said
when Lisa and I were alone in the kitchen.
'But when can we take the photos?'
'It's five o'clock,' said Lisa.
'He won't go out again today.
He'll probably be working in the cellar
for the rest of the evening.'
'It's hopeless,' I said. 'We can't do it.'
Lisa was staring blankly into the distance.
'Unless …' she said, 'unless we go in the middle
of the night. He won't hear us if he's asleep.'

We decided to risk it.
We'd get some photos and take them
to the police in the morning.
'Make it two o'clock,' I said.
'He'll be well asleep by then.'

It was hard, keeping myself awake.
I almost dropped off once or twice.
When I finally opened my bedroom door,
Lisa was already waiting on the landing.
She handed me her torch and waved the camera
to show she hadn't forgotten it.
We crept silently downstairs.

As I peered through the gloom,
I could see something waiting at the bottom …
It was Franco. He jumped up to greet us.
'What's he doing here?' I whispered to Lisa.
'He's allowed to wander around at night,'
she hissed back. 'In case of burglars.'
She petted him to keep him from whining.
I, meanwhile, tackled the front door.
It was a mess of locks, bolts and chains.

Finally I got the door open.
'Stay,' I whispered to Franco,
pointing my finger at him.
We closed the door behind us
and crept around to the cellar opening.
We slipped our fingers through the bars
and pulled. This time it gave way easily
and we dropped down into the cellar.

'We did it!' I said as I switched on the light.
We grinned at each other
and Lisa started taking photos of the plants.
'Let's get some of the rats,' I said
and headed towards the far side of the cellar.
But we weren't ready for what happened next.
One of my laces must have come undone.
Suddenly, I tripped. I fell against a table,
knocking one of the glass cases to the floor.
'We'd better get it cleared up,' said Lisa.
'With a bit of luck, he won't notice it's missing
until we've gone.'
It was while we were sweeping up the mess
that we heard the noise.

Whining. Scratching. It was Franco.

He must have heard the breaking glass.

He was at the cellar door –

the one near the kitchen.

We looked up in horror.

Now he was barking.

The professor would hear it for certain.

We had to get out.

7

Disaster Strikes

'Franco! What is it?' The professor was coming
down the stairs, calling to the dog.
We panicked. We couldn't go back inside
the house. We had to run for it.
'I'll give you a leg up,' I said to Lisa.
But, as she tried to scramble out
of the cellar, her foot slipped.
She fell back, knocking me to the ground.
My head cracked against the stone.
My leg twisted under me and I yelled
with pain. I couldn't move.

Lisa tugged my arm but it was no good.
'Try to get up, Tom,' she begged.
'I can hear him unlocking the door.'
It was hopeless. My head was spinning.
I knew it was too late.

By the time my eyes opened,
Professor Riffard was standing over me.
He kicked me in the ribs as I tried to sit up.
'You've been nosing around, have you?' he said.
I could scarcely move
but I felt the anger boil up inside.
'We know what you're up to!
We've got evidence.
You'll spend the rest of your life in the nick!'
'I don't think so!' he said.
'I think you'll spend your life in "the nick"
as you call it.'
I didn't know what he meant.
Then he pointed to the rats' cages and said,
'You'll have company, too!'
Lisa shrank back against the wall
as Riffard reached for a metal bar.

He raised it above his head.
'MOVE!' he said. Lisa had no choice but to
step towards the cages. She was terrified.
'Leave her alone!' I shouted.

He turned, gripped me by the collar
and dragged me across the floor.
When we were on the far side of the cellar,
he pressed us against the cages.
'Now!' he said as he reached for a key
and turned it in the lock.
'Enjoy your stay!' he mocked,
grabbing hold of my arm.
'Only two to a cell!'

The huge rat was glaring at me.
Its jaws were set ready to attack.
Slowly Riffard opened the door a fraction.
Then I felt his hand on my back
pushing me inside.
'NO!' I screamed and shut my eyes
as the rat leaped forward.

I waited for the pain, but nothing happened.
The great black body had flung itself
at the half closed door and knocked it open.
It latched its claws onto the professor's arm.
It sank its massive teeth into his neck.
Its attack was full of hatred.

But Riffard wasn't finished.
'No you don't!' he yelled and smashed
the metal bar across the creature's skull.
In seconds, the rat was dead at his feet.
Riffard kicked the body out of the way.
Then he leaned forward
and turned the key in the lock. I was trapped.
'Now you, my dear,' he said looking at Lisa.
This was it, I thought. No way out.
But Lisa surprised me.
'I don't think so,' she said.
Riffard stepped towards her.
'Try and get me,' she said and she moved away.
'Why you …' Furious, he stepped forward
but then he stumbled. He tried to get up.
But again he fell.
Now I could see why.

Blood was spurting from his neck.
A few moments later he was unconscious.
We were safe. Lisa unlocked the cage.
'Thanks, Lisa,' I said and hugged her.

We made our way to the cellar steps
to get help.
'Just look at that lot,' I said as we passed
a shelf full of Riffard's growth hormone.
'Think of the damage that lot could have done!'
Suddenly, I was filled with rage. I struck
out with my fist and burst one of the bags.
'Good riddance!' I said
as the powder spilled out.
But Lisa gasped in horror.
'Are you CRAZY?' she yelled,
frantically trying to scoop up the powder.
'Look what you've done!'
Then I saw. The powder was pouring
into a drain hole in the floor.
'Rats live in sewers,' she screamed.
'Use your imagination, Tom.
Don't you know what will happen next?'